KILLER VIRUS

BY R. A. MONTGOMERY

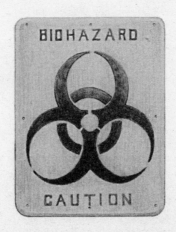

ILLUSTRATED BY ERIC CHERRY

BANTAM BOOKS
NEW YORK • TORONTO • LONDON • SYDNEY • AUCKLAND

RL 4, ages 8–12

KILLER VIRUS

A Bantam Book / May 1997

CHOOSE YOUR OWN ADVENTURE® is a registered trademark
of Bantam Books, a division of Bantam Doubleday Dell
Publishing Group, Inc.
Registered in U.S. Patent and Trademark Office
and elsewhere.

Original conception of Edward Packard

Cover art by Bill Schmidt
Interior illustrations by Eric Cherry

ISBN 0-553-56753-5
Published simultaneously in the United States and Canada

Bantam Books are published by Bantam Books, a division of
Bantam Doubleday Dell Publishing Group, Inc. Its trademark,
consisting of the words "Bantam Books" and the portrayal of a
rooster, is Registered in U.S. Patent and Trademark Office and in
other countries. Marca Registrada. Bantam Books, 1540
Broadway, New York, New York 10036.

PRINTED IN THE UNITED STATES OF AMERICA
CWO   0 9 8 7 6 5 4 3 2 1

To Janet Hubbard-Brown
for her continued
help and enthusiasm
in research and writing.

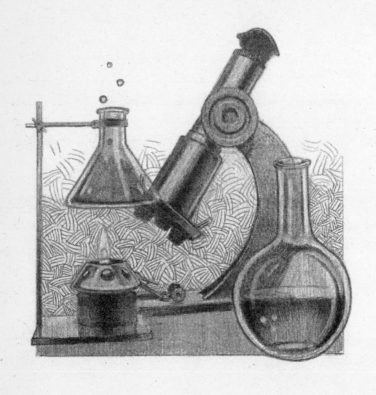

WARNING!!!

This book is not like other books you have read. In this story, *you* choose what happens next. There are many different endings, so you can read this book over and over again and it will be different every time.

As you read, you'll have the chance to decide what will happen. Whenever you make a decision, turn to the page shown. What happens to you next in the story depends on your choices.

One choice could lead you to the cure for a terrible virus. But another choice could kill you and thousands of other innocent people.

It's your choice. Your thrills. *Your* adventure!

AUTHOR'S NOTE

Ebola is a real disease that was first seen in northern Zaire, Africa, and southern Sudan in 1976. It was named after the Ebola River, a small stream of water in northern Zaire. In Zaire 318 cases of Ebola were reported in 1976 and 88 percent of those reported died. In the Sudan that same year, 53 percent of 151 cases died.

A second Ebola outbreak occurred in 1979 in Sudan. In 1989, a new strain of the Ebola virus, called Ebola Reston, broke out in a building housing monkeys to be used in laboratory experiments in Reston, Virginia. Many monkeys, but no humans, died during this outbreak.

Ebola continues to appear sporadically in West Africa. It most recently appeared in Liberia, and in 1996 a case was reported in Gabon. The person who contracted Ebola had been handling a chimpanzee that had died of the disease.

Other diseases similar to Ebola have been discovered: the Marburg virus is one, and Lassa Fever, found only in West Africa, is another.

Scientists continue to study and search for a cure for Ebola. But as yet there is no known cure.

"Is that the Nobe River down below?" you ask your uncle, who is sitting next to you on the small plane. He leans over to peer through the dusk at the winding river below. "It is indeed," he replies with a smile.

You consult your map of the continent. Your plane will land in the capital of the Republic of Nuano, a small country. From there you will continue on to Shigali, a town located fifty miles from the capital.

You feel lucky to be allowed to accompany the team of virus detectives, who are on a mission to find out why hundreds are dying from a horrible disease in the Shigali area. Your uncle is Steve Bergstein, a famous American epidemiologist—a big word for a scientist who studies epidemic diseases. "Epidemic" is a word used for a contagious disease that spreads rapidly. Uncle Steve suspects the disease is Ebola.

Just the word *Ebola* terrifies you. People who catch the disease suffer bad headaches, then their throats become so sore they can barely swallow. As they grow sicker and sicker, their symptoms become more extreme, until they are vomiting violently and bleeding around the eyes and gums. Eventually these victims lapse into a coma and die, but not before they have suffered horribly.

Your uncle and his fellow scientists are hoping to identify the disease in Shigali and then try to discover its cause. If they're lucky, they may stop its spread. There is no known cure for Ebola.

→

Working around the Ebola virus is extremely dangerous. Whether you are out in the wilderness trying to find the source of the disease, or in the city hospital tending to the sick, one small slip, such as pricking yourself with a needle, can mean death.

And as if the disease weren't enough trouble, your uncle has warned you about the warfare going on between the Republic of Nuano and the neighboring country of Chunga. The dictator of Chunga has twice sent an army to the capital of Nuano to try to take over the government. So far he hasn't succeeded, but the president of Nuano is worried. The Chungan dictator, Mojundi, is determined to expand his poorer country's boundaries and wealth by taking over Nuano, which is known to have gold mines. Mojundi will stop at nothing, and everyone knows it.

Rumors have been filtering down through the CIA that Mojundi has threatened to violate international law and use disease as a weapon. Weakening the population of Nuano by means of a virus like Ebola would make it easy to overtake the country.

As the plane circles to land, you overhear Ron Winters, one of the team's scientists, telling Uncle Steve that Mojundi's men have been secretly infiltrating the government and health council of Nuano. "What if a Mojundi soldier injected someone in Shigali with the Ebola virus? How would we know?" he asks.

"The first patient was probably bitten by a monkey

→

or some other animal that was carrying the disease," Uncle Steve scoffs. "We're not here to theorize about politics. We're here to stop the spread of a virus."

Your stomach does a flip-flop as the plane hits the runway. Leaving the plane, you gasp as the intense heat and humidity envelop you. You enter the airport, which isn't much cooler, with the rest of the team: epidemiologists like your uncle and veterinarians.

A tap on your shoulder interrupts your thoughts. Mark Turner is smiling at you and holding up a can of soda. For some reason, Mark really gets on your nerves. He's six feet four and built like a football player. He has a graying, flat-top haircut and oversized teeth that make him look as if he's going to bite you when he smiles. You know that he begged your uncle to let him come. Last year he was accused of stealing an idea from a professor at the university where he worked, but no one could prove he did it. Uncle Steve has always believed in giving people a second chance, but you think your uncle may be too nice.

"Want to finish this? Don't worry—I don't have Ebola." Mark laughs.

"No thanks," you say, shaking your head.

Mark is the most competitive scientist on this journey. He is the only scientist in the group who can easily switch roles. He is as comfortable in caves hunting bats as he is in the hospital.

Turn to page 54.

4

In a gravelly voice, Roloff says, "You have a choice." He pulls a badge out of his linen jacket. "I am a secret member of the international police force. We need you to admit you took the blood and sold it. It will give us a chance to go after Dictator Mojundi."

You're cautious. If they really are international police, and can prove that Mojundi is using the contaminated blood as a weapon, then you could help them stop the spread of a horrible disease. But why *you*?

"I didn't take the blood, though. *You* did," you reply. "You framed me." You hesitate. "And what if I *don't* do as you ask?"

Mark steps forward. "If you don't confess, we can keep you here for a very long time. If you confess, we'll have you out of here and back to safety immediately."

"So I'll be sent back to the United States?" you ask.

"You want to stay here in this mess?" Mark asks.

If you want to stay and clear your name, go to page 10.

If you agree to sign the confession, knowing you'll be safer back home, go to page 40.

You have to help Artie! Mark and Roloff are dangerous. Propped in the corner of the office you see an ancient rifle, the kind used to kill big game animals. You've never shot a gun in your life.

It makes you sad to think that your uncle fell for Mark's lies, but you have to admit how convincing he's been. The worst part is that Mark, Roloff, and Mojundi may get away with murdering thousands of people.

You grab the gun and cock it. Outside the window, you see two figures talking to Artie. Slowly and silently you open the door. Pulling the gun up to your shoulder, you aim it at one of the shadowy figures. But you don't have the nerve. You just can't kill someone, even if that person is threatening Artie.

Suddenly, to your shock, your uncle steps forward. "I didn't come all the way out here just to have you shoot my right-hand assistant," he says. Then he starts to laugh. Wes, his assistant, refuses to come any closer.

You drop the gun. Uncle Steve gives you a hug.

"What's going on?" you ask.

"Mark and Roloff—I mean Raoul—are in jail," he says. "I knew something was fishy, but I had to play along until we knew the truth for sure. Are you all right?"

"Never been better," you smile. "Thanks to Artie."

"Let's go, then. We have work to do," Uncle Steve replies.

The End

One cage contains hundreds of varieties of birds. Their colors are brilliant. You love watching the cockatoos. About two hundred parakeets fly about in an enormous cage. In a smaller cage you see about fifteen birds that look tired and not as perky as the others.

A worker approaches the cages. You're not sure why, but you duck behind a small shed to watch him. The worker takes out the sickly looking birds and hands them to another man, who places them in a cage, pays the worker, and leaves.

You walk on back to where Julia is extracting blood from a monkey. She smiles as you approach. The vials are lined up in a special container to be sent to a lab back in the city. You kneel down to help her, placing a surgical mask over your face. You tell her about the birds you saw, and how they were sold. She stares at you.

"One of the nurses at the hospital told me that many of the locals have pet parakeets," Julia says. "They believe they bring good luck."

You freeze. Could the parakeets be spreading Ebola?

"Come on," you say to Julia. "Let's find Burt."

"No. First, let's find Simon Graneur," Julia says. "I think he'll tell me the truth."

You follow Julia around the cages. The two of you find Simon over near the birds.

Turn to page 65.

Your heart is pounding, and you can hardly breathe. You run to the hot zone lab. There's a small closet where the lab suits are kept. You can hide in there.

The ultraviolet light in the room gives everything an eerie look. You crawl into the closet and close the door. *What a stupid thing to be doing,* you think. You're playing hide-and-seek with grown men who might be terrorists.

It's hot in the closet. Perspiration runs down your face. You sit for a long time and hear nothing. You have just put your hand on the doorknob to open the door when you hear a shuffling sound. Someone has entered the lab.

You listen carefully, but for a while you don't hear anything else. Then you hear a man's voice—it's Mark. But who is he talking to? Is it the stranger? Are they looking for you?

"Where do you think the kid went?" someone with a strange accent says.

"Probably scared off." That's Mark speaking. "Don't worry. Let's get suited up."

They're suiting up? They must be going in to get the contaminated blood, you realize. There are at least fifty tubes of it in there on ice. You open the door of the closet. Your hands shaking, you jam a chair under the doorknob that leads into the Level 4 lab room, barricading Mark and the stranger inside. They realize what you have done and begin pounding on the door.

Turn to page 56.

With that, Ron climbs into the driver's seat of the Land Rover and waits for you to get in. You and Maryanne follow. Ron turns the Land Rover around and bumps across the trail and down through the grass.

"I don't see anything," Maryanne says. "Oh, wait! Isn't that Mark?"

Mark is standing approximately where you left the box. Ron drives straight up to him.

"I'm glad you came back for me. Thought I'd have to spend the night out here," Mark chuckles. He climbs into the backseat with you.

Maryanne turns to him. "Did you find the box of blood samples, Mark?"

Mark turns and looks at you. He speaks to Maryanne, never taking his eyes off you. "The blood samples are back with Roloff. Now what should we do with our informer?"

Maryanne? Ron? They're in on this? You're stunned.

"Take me back to my uncle," you say, your voice tight with fear.

"Sorry. You know way too much," Ron says.

You try to reach over and open the door of the Land Rover, but Mark grabs your hands and binds your wrists with electrical tape.

"There's no escape," Maryanne says softly.

The End

You decide to stay and clear your name. These guys are probably lying about being members of the international police force anyway. "I'm not signing anything," you declare.

"Suit yourself," Mark says. They both exit, slamming the door.

You rush to the door and open it wide. A policeman is standing guard. You start to go into the hallway, but he stands in front of you and pushes you back. "Let me out!" you cry. He doesn't say a word, just gives you another push and closes the door.

This is crazy, you think. You walk over to the window and stare out. *They could leave me here forever, and no one would ever find me.*

A bright flash outside makes you jump. Artie, the obnoxious reporter, is out there. You wave your arms frantically, but he doesn't get it. He snaps another photograph. You turn away from the window and sit on the bare floor.

After a couple of hours you get up and pound on the door. The guard opens it. You demand that he take you to the bathroom. He puts handcuffs on you and leads you down the empty corridor. He unlocks the handcuffs, and you enter a small bathroom. Quickly you look around for any means of escape. The window is too high. But you notice a stack of paper towels.

Turn to page 34.

"Why not wear a disguise?" Artie asks. You see a man on the side of the road wearing a turban and a long robe. You stop and offer him some money for his clothes. He accepts, and you trade clothing.

Arriving back at the hospital, you walk up to the gate and explain in your best false accent that you are a doctor from Cairo. Before they can quiz you further, you dart through the front doors.

You see Mark and Roloff in the administration office. You go past the office and start to run. The last room on the left has your uncle's name on the door. You tiptoe in. The attending nurse gasps. Before she can stop you, you have poked the needle of the syringe filled with good serum into your uncle's upper arm.

His eyes flutter open. He doesn't say anything, but he does smile slightly. Five team members enter. You remove the turban.

Your uncle is conscious, and you tell him and the team the entire story. They believe you. Soon after you disappeared, they had begun to suspect Mark and Roloff. Uncle Steve smiles and squeezes your hand.

You leave Uncle Steve's room to let him rest, just in time to see Mark and Roloff confronted by the rest of the team.

They don't stand a chance. You turn and go back to your uncle's room, hoping the serum will work, glad that he finally knows the truth.

The End

"We can inject them tonight and head back across the border," Roloff continues. "Our plan is working well."

"What about the scientists?" one of the people sitting around the fire asks.

Roloff laughs. "Don't worry. They will be walking back to the city. I emptied the gas tank of the Land Rover before I left it!"

Good thing the idiot didn't bother to check for extra gasoline, you think.

If only you could get your hands on the blood. But Mark and the others are probably waiting for you. You creep in closer to the gathering. You see a tent with two guards standing in front. The word "Mojundi" is stamped on the front flap.

The captors seem surprisingly relaxed. They are drinking and roasting a goat. You spot the little refrigerator off to the side of the group. The generator is humming along. Slowly and carefully you creep closer to the refrigerator.

You reach up and open the door. It doesn't look as if the box containing the vials of blood and syringes has been touched. Carefully you slide the box out. Everyone continues talking. But you feel someone watching you. You glance over. It's one of the captives. Her face registers nothing. You're safe.

→

You start back the way you came. Carrying the box is difficult; the insulation makes it heavy. Just when you're far enough away to stand up and run, you see a shadowy figure coming down the path alongside the river. It stops and listens.

It's Mark! He's alone. You don't breathe. He makes his way to the campsite. There he is greeted like an old friend.

Turn to page 62.

You decide to follow the group. The captors don't know you are here—*unless* Mark tells them, in which case you will know once and for all that he's on their side. You follow them toward the lighted area.

It looks like a military camp. Three guards stand at attention. You get as close as you dare. Olive-green tents cover most of the site. One tent houses a huge kitchen where native women stand cooking over a fire. You make your way over to within hearing distance of a group of men who look like European businessmen. One of them is speaking rapidly. "It will look like an accident. We'll take care of it."

You try to find Ron and Maryanne in the large crowd of people milling about. You have to help them. Then you see them in front of one of the tents. Roloff and Mark are with them. No one seems upset, which is strange.

Maryanne puts her arm in Mark's as they walk around. *What has he told them?* you wonder. You watch as they walk together to the tent closest to you. Then Mark and Roloff wave and leave. You move a little closer. Maryanne is talking with Ron. You stick your head out and whisper loudly, "Ron! Maryanne! Come on!"

They turn. "Oh, it's you!" Maryanne says. "Everything's fine," she reassures you. "We're just playing along. Mark will get us out of here. Meet us at the Land Rover."

Turn to page 67.

16

You join the group planning to search for the source of the Ebola virus as they gather around Burt Sherman. Burt has spent many years traveling around the world investigating the origins of a variety of viruses. He is known for both his courage and his crankiness.

"Now listen up," he says gruffly. "This is no pleasure trip. We're going up to Kimundi Cave in the northern part of Nuano to see what's happening there. The first man stricken with the virus spent time in that cave just prior to becoming ill. That makes it a possible source. The virus could have come from a monkey, or a spider, or even something bigger. We'll be trapping animals and testing them.

"I want you to meet our chief veterinarian, Ms. Julia Arquette, who's come from Paris to help out. Please give her all the help she needs."

The ten members of the team load up two Land Rovers. The cave is about a day's drive away.

You notice from the window that Burt is talking with Mark Turner and another man on the hospital steps. Mark is looking over Burt's shoulder at the Land Rovers. He's pointing to yours.

You sigh. "Oh no."

"What's wrong?" Julia asks you.

"Nothing. Well, actually—" you begin. But you are interrupted by Mark's voice.

Turn to page 100.

You're willing to risk your life to try to get out of this situation now. "I'll help you load up the stuff," you say. "But I want you to know you're making a huge mistake."

"Shut up!" Mark explodes. "Just do what I say. Put the squirrel in the Land Rover!"

"The squirrel?" you ask innocently.

Roloff walks over. "Do as he says."

"I will. I will," you reply. "But why do you want the squirrel?"

"It's the host," Mark says, seething.

"Are you sure?" you ask. "Excuse me, Julia, but that wasn't the squirrel's blood you just did, was it?"

Julia looks very cool and collected. "No." She starts mixing all the vials around. "But which one was it? Mark, you frightened me so, I'm confused."

Mark looks furious. "You're both going to die," he says, "unless you hand me the blood containing the virus."

You really *are* confused now. There was no time to label anything. The blood is completely mixed up. A loud crackling comes over the radio in the Land Rover. "Town to Cave. Can you read me?"

Mark motions for you to reply. "Go ahead," you say into the radio.

Turn to page 72.

18

"What did he say?" you ask.

Mark shrugs. "Something about us bringing bad luck," he replies.

Ron speaks up. "This village has to be quarantined." He turns to the translator, who tells the chief. The chief nods, then says that your group should stay in the village, too. The translator informs him that more help will be coming. The chief offers to send two of his men with you, but you tell him you'll be fine on your own.

The sun is setting as you begin to hike out. You follow the same path the mysterious Land Rover thief took. Before you've walked an hour, you see the metal of the Land Rover glinting in the moonlight. Mark seems nervous.

Everyone is excited to see the Land Rover. But it seems abandoned. You can't help wondering where the stranger went.

Ron looks in the back of the Land Rover. The little refrigerator containing the vials of blood has disappeared.

"Where is the creep, and why did he take off with the blood?" he shouts. "This is really bad news."

Mark tries to be reassuring, but you have chills. "Oh, Ron," he says. "Stop being so paranoid. I think the guy was drunk."

You notice footprints in the muddy grass. "Look!" you shout. "We could follow these prints!"

Turn to page 94.

You decide to hide in the closet. Moments after you pull the door closed behind you, you hear voices entering Artie's office.

The talking drones on and on. You've never been this hot in your life. Your whole body feels wet with sweat. Just when you think you can't stand another second here in the closet, you realize that all is quiet. You must have dropped off to sleep.

You unlatch the door and quietly crawl out of the closet. You lie for a few minutes on the cool linoleum floor. You see a bottle of water on Artie's desk. Slowly you get up and take a few sips. It's dark out.

You drink some more water and think about what to do next. You should probably get back to the hospital and find your uncle. What if he still thinks you are selling bad blood?

You're scared to turn on the office lights, but you find a flashlight in Artie's desk. You flick it on and cast the light around the room. You shine it on a stack of papers on Artie's desk, then move it over to the fax machine. You notice that a fax has just come in.

Curious, you pull it out of the machine and read it. It's from the Paris office of the international police network. Your hand begins trembling as you read. The fax says that the man calling himself Roloff Boulin is not a virologist but an international terrorist.

That's it. You've got to get back to the hospital! Who knows what happened to Artie?

Turn to page 48.

"That reporter could start a worldwide panic," you tell Mark, annoyed at the way he joked around.

"Who cares?" Mark demands. He takes the vial of blood from your hands. "If this is a new strain of virus, and if I discover that in the lab," he says sarcastically, "then I'll become famous, won't I?"

"My uncle thinks it's Ebola," you reply, taking the tube back from him. "And *I'll* do the lab test."

"Let's suit up," Mark says. "You go first."

You enter the specially sterilized changing room, remove your old surgical scrubs, and put on a fresh, sterile surgical suit. Next you put on a cloth surgical cap, clean white socks, and rubber surgical gloves. Then you begin taping the cuffs of your gloves to the sleeves of your scrub suit and your socks to your pants. Your final step is to put on the pressurized, heavy-duty plastic space suit worn in the lab to protect against contaminated blood or disease-carrying agents. The gloves attached to the suit are made of heavy rubber. You plug a yellow hose into the suit—it will supply you with oxygen—and the suit puffs up. Then you enter the lab and wait for Mark to suit up.

It's uncomfortable being in such tight quarters with Mark, especially when you're working with such dangerous material. But you have no choice. Testing on the blood samples needs to begin right away.

Turn to page 96.

You and Julia decide to join the group that will check out the nearby zoo. You'll leave the next day.

Julia leaves your side to get some of the goat stew that has been cooking over the fire. Mark and Roloff wander across to where you're sitting alone. Roloff speaks in his so-called French accent: "We go where you go. We have to keep an eye on young scientists who aren't always sure what they're doing."

The following day you hike into the bush with the others. Soon your group reaches the home of Simon Graneur, who owns the zoo. The *caw-cawing* of caged birds and the constant *kra-kra-kra* sounds made by the monkeys is almost deafening.

Simon rushes from his home to greet you. A runner has gone ahead to inform him of your arrival. He seems friendly enough, but there is a nervousness about him—or is it fear? He keeps looking over at Roloff, who doesn't take his eyes off him.

Turn to page 28.

The box of contaminated blood is brought to the fire. The medicine man throws the vials into the fire, one by one. Each time, the villagers chant. The medicine man points to you again. The chief says something, and the giant turns to you and asks if you have anything to say.

You speak slowly in English. "My uncle is Steve Bergstein, a famous doctor. He is at the hospital in Shigali now, working with the sick people there. There is only one among us who is working with the evil dictator Mojundi."

When the natives hear that name, loud shouting begins. The chief puts up his arm to stop them.

"I knew nothing until last night," you explain quietly.

"You must pay," the chief says.

The medicine man steps forward. He leads you over piles of twigs to a large wooden post. One of the villagers approaches the mound of kindling with a torch lit from the bonfire. The medicine man puts a blindfold over your eyes and ties you to the post. Everyone grows silent.

You hear someone shouting in the distance. It sounds like your uncle. But the crackling of twigs catching fire drowns out any other sound. You feel the heat of the first flames licking at your legs.

Suddenly someone is untying you and lifting you over the small flames. It's a policeman. Your uncle runs up and embraces you.

Turn to page 66.

Ron is staring at you, his face expressionless. "Now try to tell us what you ran into," he says.

You take a deep breath and explain about the people around the campfire and the captives. "I had the contaminated blood with me until a quarter of a mile back there," you explain.

Ron looks skeptical. "You're saying that Mojundi's people are back there at a campfire about to inject contaminated blood into natives of this country?"

You nod. You realize that Ron and Maryanne doubt your story.

"Are you implying that Mark is part of this horrible operation?" Maryanne asks.

Nodding again, you tell about seeing his shadow moving swiftly along the riverbank. "I think he might try to kill me. He threatened to kill Ron," you say.

"Maybe we should go back and try to find the box of contaminated blood. And Mark," says Ron.

"He'll know I told you. I think he's capable of killing us all in order to avoid getting caught."

Ron laughs. "What movies have you been watching lately?"

Maryanne looks stern. "We have to try to get the blood samples. If what you are saying is true, they can wipe out a community in no time."

"You have to trust us," Ron adds. "We can handle Mark."

Turn to page 8.

"I think we should follow the tracks," you say. Ron takes the flashlights out of the Land Rover. It's obvious that Mark is furious and not going to cooperate.

Maryanne gets behind Ron, who is moving quickly ahead. It's easy to follow the footprints because the ground near the river is marshy. Mark comes up behind you and whispers harshly in your ear, *"Don't say anything."*

"We've got a good chance of catching him," Ron puffs. "He doesn't know we're after him." The trail is harder to follow now as it leads farther into the deep jungle.

Maryanne stops for a second. "Wait. What do you propose we do when we catch him?"

"What if he has a weapon?" you ask.

"We'll deal with that problem when we come to it," Ron asserts. You want to laugh. It's hard to imagine Ron dealing with a criminal. But the seriousness of your situation weighs on you, too. If these people really are in a conspiracy to infect a country with the Ebola virus, they will stop at nothing.

The canopy of trees has almost completely blocked out the moonlight. Suddenly you stop. A loud chattering breaks the silence of the jungle: *Kra! Kra!* you hear over and over.

"There are lights up ahead," Maryanne says.

"Let's go!" Ron starts running.

Turn to page 44.

26

"Every minute counts," you say. Artie drives as fast as he can, and you finally reach a small cluster of thatched huts. The mosquitoes are so bad that they cover your whole body. Artie boldly drives into the village center. You both get out of the car. The chief of the village walks over, a serious expression on his face.

He speaks a little English. Artie asks about the illness. The chief takes you to a hut behind all the others, where the sick have been quarantined. He wears no protection.

You return with the chief to his big hut. Inside, his wife is preparing goat stew. It smells delicious. She offers you some, and both you and Artie accept. Then Artie tries to explain the problem—who your uncle is, and his need for antibodies.

The chief's wife gets up and smiles, pointing to herself. What luck! You ask her for one vial of her blood. She grows very frightened but finally agrees. You go to the car, get the supplies, and bring them in.

The chief tells you, through a few words in English and pantomime, that two people in his village have survived. That is an amazing record. They call in one of their cured tribesmen. He allows you to take one vial of blood from him.

Now you have to figure out how to get the blood to your uncle. How can you enter the hospital? They still think you're the blood thief.

Turn to page 11.

You think fast. You could never get to Ron and Maryanne and the others in time to warn them. Though the sickness hasn't been diagnosed, you are pretty certain the people in this village are suffering from Ebola. Why else would Mark be planning to steal the blood? He could have an entire storehouse filled with blood samples! What if he's selling the blood to some government?

The stranger's voice breaks in. "If you leave with the truck they'll know what you're up to. The entire international police network will be searching for you."

"True," Mark says.

"I'll steal the truck with the blood and the radio," the stranger continues.

Mark's voice sounds edgy. "And I have to go back with these guys?"

The stranger's voice grows steely. "Get out of the truck."

You don't know what to do. You have to stop the man from taking those tubes of blood. Maybe if you hang onto the back of the Land Rover until he stops . . . but then what?

There's only one thing to do.

You walk right up to the truck. Both men are so shocked to see you that they are speechless.

"Hi, guys," you say, trying to sound nonchalant.

"Where'd you come from?" Mark asks.

Turn to page 90.

It turns out that Simon has been collecting animals to sell for years. Many of the captured animals are on their way to the West to be put into zoos. Others are held here because their parents were shot by game hunters. Julia gets her equipment ready and asks you to assist. Blood has to be drawn from a large number of the animals to see if any of them are carrying the Ebola virus.

Mark and Roloff are working nearby. At noon everyone takes a break. Not in the mood to rest, you pick up a stick and walk around the huge caged area that holds the animals. There are chimps and gorillas, snakes in glass aquariums, and flying squirrels.

Turn to page 6.

You land, along with two other helicopters carrying soldiers and other members of Uncle Steve's team. You lead everyone down the path you traveled the night before.

You rush onto the campsite. There's not a soul in sight. There are tents all around, but they seem to be deserted. One of the soldiers calls out. You follow your uncle to a large tent, and there they are! Ron and Maryanne are sitting in the tent, just staring at you.

"Are you okay?" Uncle Steve asks.

Maryanne seems in a trance. "Mark left with them," she whispers. "They shot us up with the virus."

Uncle Steve turns to you. "This is a hot zone," he says. "Get everyone out."

"But Maryanne—"

Your uncle shakes his head. "Do as I say. Get the protective gear out of the helicopters," he commands. He turns to Maryanne and Ron. "You'll be our human guinea pigs," he says. "We have some immune plasma here, which we'll inject into you now. Maybe it will work."

Turn to page 76.

They've seen you. You'd better run. You take off. Glancing back over your shoulder, you see the stranger dart out of the room. You run past the lab, hoping you're headed in the right direction.

Mark is calling your name. There's an exit door on your left. You push it open and run outside. The heat is sweltering. You'll have to get lost in the crowd.

You stop for a second to catch your breath. Turning, you are surprised to see they're not following you. Maybe they meant no harm, and you're just being paranoid.

You decide to go back to the hospital and find Uncle Steve and the rest of the team. It's time to tell your uncle, no matter how busy he is, about what you've seen. You're worried that Mark may be planning to steal the contaminated blood to use as a weapon.

Entering the hospital, you see a nurse rush by. You also see Artie, the reporter, leaning against the wall. You wonder how he got back into the hospital. Then you notice dozens of local police trying to control the flow of people in and out of the hospital.

You pick up a clean mask off the desk and walk down the corridor. Your uncle is approaching with a determined stride. The mask across his face does not hide the fury in his eyes.

"Where have you been?" he demands.

"I had to get out," you say softly. "And I need to talk with you now."

Turn to page 92.

After visiting six other patients, Maryanne and Uncle Steve are whispering. "What do you think?" she asks.

He replies, "You were at the last epidemic. The symptoms match."

"Ebola?" she asks, still whispering. He nods.

"We'll quarantine the hospital now," Uncle Steve announces. "We don't know it's Ebola, but just in case . . ."

It will be difficult to keep people out of the hospital, since the custom here is for family members to stay with patients and help out. Uncle Steve tells the nurse to make sure all family members present in the hospital be given gowns, masks, and gloves. He orders all new patients being brought in to be taken to another wing of the building.

When Maryanne is alone, you approach her. "How did they stop the last epidemic?" you ask.

"We didn't have a treatment," she recalls. "But we sterilized everything and wouldn't allow family members to touch each other. We also quarantined the village where the outbreak started."

"Was Mark there then?" you ask.

She looks surprised. "Yes, he was," she answers. "Why?"

"What happened to all the blood you collected then?" you continue.

Turn to page 61.

You grab the back of the Land Rover and hang on. Mark is shouting something, but you can't hear him over the roar of the motor. Roloff is driving fast, but somehow you are able to hold on. You don't think he has seen you. The Land Rover starts to slow down, and you manage to crawl onto the roof. Now what?

You don't know how dangerous Roloff is. If he kills you, there will be an international stir. Your uncle will see to that.

The Land Rover stops. You lie flat on the roof, barely breathing. What is Roloff doing? The door of the vehicle slams. You roll over ever so slightly toward the edge of the roof, but you cannot see him. You hear him swear as he opens the back of the Land Rover and begins to shove gear around, looking for something. He must have a flat tire.

Suddenly you hear him grunt in surprise. "Hey!" He is talking to *you*. Terrified, you lift your head slightly. He is looking directly at you.

"Don't get near me," you say.

"You're in big trouble," he answers.

You leap up, prepared to jump. "*You'll* be in big trouble if you hurt me!" you yell at him.

"But you could be dead. It would take months for anyone to find you out here. What if you get . . . Ebola?" he asks, a cruel smile on his face. He starts to climb up onto the roof of the Land Rover. You notice that he has something in his hand.

Turn to page 82.

You return to the guard with a wad of paper towels in your pocket. How to get a pencil or pen? You feel around in your pockets for money. You act out writing a letter to the guard, then show him the money. He shakes his head, but when you get back to the room where you're being held, you hold up the money again. The guard hesitates. He reaches in his pocket, brings out a pencil, and hands it to you. You give him all your money.

Quickly you sit down, pull out the paper, and write a note. "To Whom It May Concern: I am being held prisoner by two men who claim to be members of the international police force. They are trying to destroy all efforts to stop the spread of the Ebola virus. Their names are Mark Turner and Roloff Boulin." At the bottom you print, "Please have CIA check their identities." You roll up the paper and stick it through a small hole in the window. You sit down to wait. You realize that no one may ever see the note.

Mark returns to your cell. "I have some sad news for you," he says. "It seems that your Uncle Steve has come down with the virus."

You grab his arm. "Let me go to him," you cry. "What about antibodies? Don't you have blood from survivors that contains antibodies?" It has never been proven that antibodies in the blood of Ebola survivors can cure an infected patient, but you want them to try this treatment on your uncle.

Turn to page 50.

Finally the outline of a village appears as though it were a mirage. Children are running around a campfire playing. Women are grinding maize on stones. All the activity stops as you approach.

Mark puts up his hand in a friendly salute and walks up to the women. He gestures and points back to you. You get out with Ron and Maryanne and walk over. The other researchers wait next to the Land Rover.

Maryanne smiles and brings out some scarves and trinkets and hands them to the women. Your translator, who hasn't said a word the whole way, now looks at the women and begins to speak, pointing first to you, then to the others.

You see the women's faces crease into worried expressions. One of them rises and motions for you to follow. She leads you, the translator, Mark, and Ron into a large, thatched hut where three men are sitting.

They motion for you to sit. The translator explains why you are here. An older man, who seems to be the chief of the village, says that the sickness came three weeks ago. One of the villagers had crossed the border to Chunga to see a relative. He was caught by one of Mojundi's border police and held captive for a week. The villager related that he had slept most of the time in a cell—he thought the police were using drugs to knock him out. One week after he returned to the village, he developed a headache and finally died an awful death.

Turn to page 45.

You feel awful. All this time, Mark's weird behavior had a good explanation, but you just assumed he was one of the bad guys.

Your uncle organizes a rescue mission the following morning and asks you to be a part of it. You lead a team of soldiers back and search for the campsite. But it's no longer there. Mark Turner is never found.

The End

"But—"

"I don't have time for this now," your uncle says. "Save it until later."

You're really mad at Mark now. Eventually he catches up with the rest of the group, chatting with Maryanne as though nothing had happened.

"Let's go," Maryanne announces. "Our car is here." You walk out into the hot, damp night air. After about ten seconds, your skin feels drenched. You start to mop furiously at your sweaty face.

Uncle Steve laughs. "Get used to it," he says. He leads the way to a beat-up old Land Rover. The driver gets out and takes your luggage. A newer model is parked right behind the old one. You and Uncle Steve climb into the older vehicle along with Mark and Maryanne. The others get in the second truck. You suddenly feel exhausted. It's hard to believe you were in London only two days ago.

The driver takes you to a small hotel three blocks from the hospital. You all pile out and go inside to register.

While you wait and watch the luggage, Mark comes over to you. "Hey, my bark is much worse than my bite. Ask anyone here." Maryanne overhears him and laughs.

"It's true," she says. "Mark wouldn't hurt a flea."

Somehow you really doubt that's the case. But you smile and accept the apparent apology.

Turn to page 53.

You turn around to see if you're being followed. You aren't . . . yet. "Artie," you say, "how did you know I was in trouble? I don't know how to thank you."

"I've had my eye on those two," Artie replies. "I've been thinking for a few days that the ugly one was an imposter. I got your note, by the way. I figured they were going to kill you."

You gulp. "You lost a good story, huh?"

"You got it. This one might be almost as good, though."

Looking over at him, you manage to laugh for the first time in days. "Glad I could be of service." You tell Artie about your plan to try to find blood with antibodies from a survivor in one of the villages. He agrees it's the best thing to do, even though the chances it will work are pretty slim. The problem is, you don't have any medical supplies with which to take blood.

"No problem," Artie replies. "Open the glove compartment."

You do. Inside is a full medical kit, including vials and a couple of syringes!

"You never know when you might need medical supplies," Artie grins.

You drive on the bumpiest, ruttiest roads you've ever seen. Artie thinks he knows just the village to check out. "It's a little village called Tungi," he says. "Probably another hour from here."

Turn to page 26.

No matter what, you have to save the blood! Desperately seeking a hiding place, you run toward a clump of trees with the box in your hands.

I'm dead, you think.

Suddenly, without any warning, you are swept up into the arms of something gigantic. Too shocked to call out, you hold on tightly to the box and close your eyes. Whatever is holding you moves swiftly through the jungle. The only sound you hear is that of huge feet beating against the earth. Finally you come to a stop and are placed on the ground.

Looking up in the moonlight, you make out a very muscular person at least seven feet tall. He motions for you to follow him. You can barely keep up with his giant strides. He takes the box from you and puts it under his arm. You follow him, knowing that if you try to run away he'll easily catch you. After walking for what seems like hours, you are back at the village where you took the blood samples.

It is nearly daylight. The village chief sits near the fire, calmly waiting. A woman hands you something that looks like a pancake. You wolf it down hungrily. The giant man squats next to the chief.

The chief begins speaking. The tall man, who is apparently one of the villagers, and who speaks good English, translates. "So you are playing games with our neighboring dictator?" he asks.

"One of our scientists is a traitor," you say.

Turn to page 70.

40

You decide you'll be safer signing the confession and going back home. Mark and Roloff leave the room to get the form. Once you're back in the States, you think, you have friends who can help you. You walk over to the dirty window. Artie is standing outside. He taps on the window. You try to raise it, but it's stuck.

He's trying to tell you something. You wipe some of the dirt off the window. He's writing on a pad. He holds the pad up to the window. You can barely make out his scribbling. It says, *They're out front announcing that you're signing a confession. A dangerous thing to do. The city will kill you.*

Help me! you write with your finger on the dusty window.

He makes an "okay" sign and disappears. You hear footsteps and quickly rub your message from the windowpane. Mark and Roloff enter, papers in hand.

You feel dizzy. You haven't eaten in some time, and this whole experience has you pretty freaked out. *I'm not going to faint,* you tell yourself. You try to catch yourself as you begin sinking to the floor. You can hear noise and voices above you, but nothing that you are hearing makes any sense. The coolness of the concrete floor feels good. Mark and Roloff argue, then leave, slamming the door.

→

Just as you're regaining consciousness, you hear the door opening and shutting softly. It's Artie. You try to stand up. Artie comes over and practically lifts you off the floor.

"Listen to the crowd out there," he says. "That sound is the roar of the people. They've been told you started this epidemic."

Turn to page 99.

You decide to get out as fast as you can. Hopefully you will be able to get back to the city and Uncle Steve and bring back help. In order to find your way back when you return, you take out your Swiss army knife and carefully carve Xs in the trees leading out.

You are relieved to see the Land Rover exactly where you left it. Another thought comes to you. Quickly you pry off one of the Land Rover's hubcaps and prop it against the lone acacia tree nearby. You hop into the truck and get it started. You get back on the road and speed all the way back to the city.

It's morning when you finally arrive. You tear into the hospital and ask for Uncle Steve. You tell him and the rest of the team about what has been going on.

"We need a helicopter!" Uncle Steve commands someone. He turns back to you. "Good work. The international police have been trying to find that headquarters for weeks."

Soon after, you board a helicopter with your uncle and two members of the international police force. The helicopter flies low over the terrain you've just crossed. "Is this it?" they keep asking. Finally you spot the lone acacia tree in the middle of the grassy area where the Land Rover was parked. The hubcap is just where you left it, like a shiny dime in the vastness of the grassland. The pilot swoops down.

Turn to page 29.

"Hold on!" Mark calls suddenly. Ron stops in his tracks. "We don't know what we're getting into," Mark goes on. "My strong suggestion is that we head back and bring in reinforcements."

The chattering grows louder. Maryanne and Ron hesitate. They look puzzled. "We'll never find this place again," Maryanne says.

Quietly Mark says, "I didn't want to tell you this, but I have no choice. I'm with the CIA. I'm in a big undercover operation. Here's my badge to prove it." He pulls a wallet out of his pocket and shows you his CIA credentials.

Maryanne is obviously stunned. "Well, Mark, I couldn't be more shocked than if you told me you were working for . . . Mojundi."

Now Mark looks shocked. "Is that what you've been thinking?"

"That was a joke," says Maryanne.

"What's going on over there?" Ron points to the lights ahead.

"I think it's the headquarters of Mojundi's people," Mark says flatly. "The guy who stole the truck is one of their top agents. Roloff is the name he goes by."

"Did they start this epidemic?" Maryanne asks. "If they did, they're monsters."

Turn to page 52.

The chief goes on to say that the villagers burned the body but within another two weeks two more people came down with the disease.

"Did your tribesman handle any animals?" Ron asks.

"Of course," the chief replies. "The man captured many species of animals that he sold to importers."

Mark asks if you can see the sick villagers. The chief says that first he must consult his *nganga,* or medicine man. "He is very suspicious, because the six who went to the hospital have died," the chief says.

One of the women arrives with the nganga. He walks directly over to Ron and starts shouting. "He says his villagers are better off with *his* medicine," the translator explains. But the medicine man does agree to take you to the other sick villagers.

You slap at mosquitoes as you follow the nganga along a crooked path. A low moan draws your attention. You all stop in your tracks. A young woman is lying under an acacia tree, in the high grasses surrounding the trail. She is curled up on her side, holding her stomach. Flies swarm over her.

The two women guides run to her. "Don't go near her!" Ron shouts. He holds them back. Your translator runs back down the trail in the opposite direction.

You take off your backpack and quickly pull out the protective garb you're supposed to wear—a plastic gown and a mask. Next, you locate syringes in your bag.

Turn to page 78.

You have to get to the hot zone lab and find the blood that contains the antibodies. Out of breath and trembling with fright, you enter the back door of the hospital near your "cell." The corridor is empty. You can see the sign on the door that says Caution. Biohazard. Do Not Enter Without Badge. *What a joke,* you think.

You open the door and enter the familiar space. You breathe deeply a few times to slow yourself down so you won't make any mistakes. Donning the surgical gear, then the space suit, you slowly open the door leading to the Level 4 area. Crossing immediately to the lab refrigerator, you open the door and gasp. Most of the blood is gone. And most of the people in the hospital believe you took it! If it takes the rest of your life, you will prove that you didn't.

But what about your uncle? Carefully you take out the six vials that are sitting upright in a holder. Each is labeled Ebola. Squatting down, you peer into every corner. Propped up against the back of the refrigerator is one lone tube. Why isn't it marked?

You take it out and hold it for a couple of minutes. It *has* to be the blood with the antibodies. Rushing out of the lab, you go quickly through decontamination and back out into the hall. You see people at the far end of the corridor. Increasing your stride, you head for the administration office.

You ask the nurse there where Steve Bergstein is. From the way she is staring at you, you know you must look insane. You are wearing a pair of shorts and a T-shirt. You're wet with sweat, and you are holding a vial of blood.

Turn to page 86.

You open the front door, ready to leave. Two men emerge from a car out front and walk up to you. "Hello," they say ominously. "Remember us?"

"Roloff" is holding the confession sheet in his hand. He pushes you back into the office and turns on the lights. Mark leads you over to Artie's desk. "Sign it," he says, steel in his voice.

"Where's Artie?" you ask.

"On his way back to the States with a great story," Mark replies. "Now sign it."

You take the pen and sign.

The End

You retreat quickly, but not before they see you. You don't know who this guy is, but he's obviously not good news. He's not a member of your team and therefore could be someone very dangerous. You wish you had told Uncle Steve about the guy before, but in all the excitement of setting up the lab, you forgot.

There's no time now to think. This guy—and Mark—could spell deep trouble. You can either duck back into the lab and hide, or you can run for it, hopefully finding your uncle in the process.

If you go back to the lab and hide, go to page 7.

If you decide to run for it, go to page 30.

50

Mark is unruffled. "What makes you think your uncle automatically gets the antibodies? Do you think he deserves them more than the hundreds of others who are dying?"

"He *must* live!" you cry. "He's the one who's trying to save their lives."

"What if we don't want their lives saved?" Mark asks offhandedly.

That's it. The rage in you spills over. You attack Mark with the pencil you're holding, slamming its point into his arm. He is surprised by the pain, and you have a few seconds to dart across the floor. A flash goes off in your face. It's the reporter! "Artie!" you yell. "Get me out of here!"

The guard has disappeared. Artie grabs your arm, and the two of you run down the hallway and out a back door. Artie jumps into a Porsche that has seen better days. You hurl yourself in behind him. Artie roars through the streets. A *ping* behind you makes you turn around. Mark is shooting at you!

Turn to page 59.

"We don't know that for sure," says Mark. "If they did, what did they use to start it? I'm interested in finding out if they have discovered the source of the virus. So far, we don't know where Ebola originates. The medicine man at the village tells us their people were kidnapped and injected with the Ebola virus. But we don't know where they got it from."

While they are deciding what to do, you walk away from the group. You feel more confused than ever. Why did Mark wait until now to tell you all this? It still bothers you that he was taking money in the airport. If he *is* with the CIA, though, it would explain a lot.

You hear muffled noises and duck behind a bush. Peering out, you see Ron, Maryanne, and Mark surrounded by three men. They are led off toward the lights. The captors must not know you're here. You follow a short distance behind.

You recognize Roloff immediately. He and Mark are bringing up the rear. They stop for a moment. You see Mark trying to explain his way out of the predicament. Then the group continues on.

You are alone in the jungle. You don't know whether to follow the group or head back to the village or the city for help.

If you decide to follow the trail out and try to get help, turn to page 43.

If you decide to follow the group, turn to page 15.

You have your own room. The bathroom is down the hall. The hotel is clean but definitely not what you would call luxurious.

You fall into bed. An antiquated fan buzzes rhythmically. The next thing you know, it's daylight, and Uncle Steve is knocking on your door.

He smiles when you answer. "Come on, we have work to do." *How can he be so calm?* you wonder.

The rest of the team is waiting downstairs. Outside your hotel, the streets of Shigali are filled with garbage. A large rat runs across the road in front of you. Maryanne explains that garbage is only picked up twice a week, which is one reason disease spreads so quickly.

As you walk toward the hospital, you ask Maryanne the question that has bothered you ever since Ron Winters mentioned it on the plane. "Do you think dictators would really use a disease like Ebola as a weapon?"

"I doubt it," she replies.

Ron Winters interjects, "Don't be too sure. It sounds like science fiction. But why not? Freeze the blood of dying patients and store it, and you have a lethal weapon." You shudder at the idea.

Uncle Steve is not just an epidemiologist but also a virologist—someone who studies viruses. He talks about viruses as though they were human. They fill him with awe. "Imagine something that tiny having the power to wipe out a whole village."

Turn to page 84.

54

The airport is crowded with people and carts wheeling in and out. Travelers are calling for taxis. You meet the rest of the team members in the baggage area where boxes of supplies for the hospital are being unloaded along with the suitcases. There are at least a hundred disposable syringes, plastic gloves, surgeons' gowns, and vials for storing the blood that will be shipped to the Centers for Disease Control in Atlanta, Georgia, for testing. Some of the blood will also be shipped to labs in Europe.

The team's plan is to set up a hot zone laboratory in the main Shigali hospital, where patients' blood can be tested on the spot. The "hot zone" is the name for the area in which the virus has struck and probably still lives. That means whoever enters the hot zone lab has to be well protected. You have been in a hot zone lab before, which means you might get the opportunity to work as an assistant in this one.

Mark is standing by himself against a wall opposite the baggage area. Uncle Steve tells you to stay out of the way for the time being and to wait with Mark. Although you'd rather not, you go over to him. "Better go help the others," he says.

$\longrightarrow$

"My uncle told me to wait here with you," you reply.

Mark seems nervous. "Here," he says, shoving a wad of the local currency into your hand. "Run over there and buy me a bottled water. Quick."

"Over there" is all the way across the airport. Sighing, you take the money from Mark and start walking toward the booths where bottled water, soft drinks, and sandwiches are sold.

Turn to page 74.

56

You run out into the hallway to get help. Where is everybody? You race to the other end of the hospital. Two men come out of a room. They scream at you, "Get out!"

"Where's the team?" you ask.

One of them lifts you up and starts running for the door.

"Bomb explosion. Terrorists," he gasps. "Where were you?"

Before you can answer, there is a giant explosion. Rubble rains down all around you. You fall to the ground and cover your head. You look back in horror. The entire wing containing the hot zone lab—and its deadly contents—has been blown sky-high.

The End

Mark is smirking. "On their word alone?" you ask your uncle. You can't believe this is happening.

One of the team scientists speaks up. "We are in the process of trying to stop an epidemic." Wearily he continues, "You'll be kept at the other end of the hospital for interrogation. Then they'll move you down to police headquarters if necessary. It would be preferable not to have this drama go outside these walls."

You feel as if you're in the middle of a nightmare. One of the policemen steps forward and tells you to follow him. Humiliated, you do as he says.

You're led back to the vacant part of the hospital where you saw Mark and Roloff talking before. *So that guy is a famous virologist? If he really is, I'll eat smoked monkey meat,* you declare to yourself.

The policeman locks you inside a bare room. There is a small, dirty window, a bed with no mattress, and a hard-backed chair. The policeman tells you in broken English that he will remain outside the door. If you need to use the bathroom, you'll have to knock.

You sit in the chair and try to think. Within half an hour there is a knock at the door. Mark and Roloff enter. You turn away, furious and a little frightened.

Turn to page 4.

"Which way?" Artie asks.

"We have to get blood with antibodies for my uncle," you tell him.

You remember the few vials of good blood at the hospital, but Mark and Roloff may have stolen them. The only way to find out is to go back there. Your only other alternative is to go out to a village and try to find someone who was infected with the virus and then cured . . . but that might take too much time.

If you decide going back to the hospital is too risky, and want to try the village, go to page 38.

If you decide to circle back to the hospital to find blood with antibodies, go to page 80.

60

Uncle Steve hands you a vial of blood that he has just taken from the dying man. He asks you to rush it to the lab. The moment you reach out your hand to take the vial, a flashbulb goes off in your face, and you nearly drop it. Your uncle starts screaming at a photographer who has just entered the room, wearing only a mask for protection. Before you can stop him, the photographer reaches over and takes a picture of the dying patient. "Get out of here!" your uncle bellows, knocking the camera out of his hand. You lead the photographer out.

"My name is Artie," he says to you. "I'm a journalist. This is worse than they're letting out, huh?"

You don't answer him. How in the world did a journalist get into the hospital?

"You believe Mojundi started this?" he asks.

"I don't know," you reply sternly. You round the bend to the lab and bump into Mark. Artie runs up to him. "Aren't you the virus chaser, Mark Turner? Will you give me a statement?"

"What kind of statement?" Mark asks, almost laughingly. "That there is a major epidemic here and that people are freaking out that—what's-his-name? Oh, yes, Mojundi—started it? It's all nonsense. How did you get in here anyway? Excuse me."

You escort Artie to the entrance of the hospital, where the guards make sure that he leaves. Then you return to the lab, where you find Mark.

Turn to page 20.

"Mark was in charge of collecting and sending the blood off to the labs," she replies. "He's the expert in this business. Aren't you, Mark?" she adds. Mark has appeared as quietly as a shadow behind you.

"I'm a vampire—didn't you know?" Mark laughs.

After a long, exhausting day, the entire team meets for dinner in the hotel restaurant. Uncle Steve makes an announcement. "Time is of the essence," he says in a serious tone. "I've decided to divide us up. There are three areas where our expertise is needed. More team members will be arriving tomorrow."

He continues, "Some of you will go to the outlying villages. There's one in particular that many of the sick have come from. Another group can stay here at the hospital with me and work with patients. It'll be tough, dealing with so many dying. And a few of you will be asked to go out and try to find the carrier of this disease. It could be the tiniest insect, or a bigger mammal. We don't know."

"And what if it isn't a virus?" one of the researchers asks.

"Then we'll all go home," Uncle Steve says. "I don't think that will happen, though. From all we've seen, this looks like a virus."

You glance around. Maybe you'll watch and see what Mark does. You know you don't want to be working with him. On the other hand, it might be good to keep an eye on him.

Turn to page 79.

You have to get back to the Land Rover. You hold the box close under your right arm and take off through the grass so you don't run into Mark. There is no path. Luckily you have a good sense of direction.

You hear shouting behind you. You think you see the lights of the Land Rover ahead.

The voices are growing louder. The box is slowing you down. If you drop it, you'll have a chance of making it to the Land Rover and safety. If you don't, your chance of being captured increases tremendously.

If you decide to drop the box in order to make it to the Land Rover, turn to page 73.

If you choose to carry the box of blood with you, no matter what happens, turn to page 39.

It's a good thing you didn't lock the squirrel's cage. Wearing gloves, you gently pick the little creature up and place it back in the cage. At least it survived. You'll need it for further testing.

The End

"Mr. Graneur?" Julia asks politely. "I'd like to withdraw blood from the parakeets now. Do you recall selling parakeets to any villagers around the town of Shigali?"

Simon Graneur looks panicked. "No!" he says emphatically. "Tomorrow, though, I go to Shigali with pet birds." He has to shout above the noise the birds are making.

Suddenly Mark's voice interrupts. "Simon, you heard the lady. She wants to check out the birds." Mark grabs Julia's arm, someone grabs yours, and when you turn, you are face-to-face with Roloff. Suddenly you realize where you have seen him before. He's the man Mark was talking to at the airport!

Before you can cry for help, Mark and Roloff have opened the door to one of the enormous birdcages and pushed you in.

"Mr. Graneur—please help us!" you beg.

"It doesn't pay to be nosy," he replies.

Something nips at your head. You try to swat it off. Another bird darts down and bites your arm. You hear Julia screaming. The sick birds are attacking you! But you know no one can hear your cries over those of the birds.

Your arm is bleeding as you grab Julia. She calls out to you, "Ebola! This could be the source!" You scream for help again. But no one hears you.

The End

"Ron and Maryanne told us everything," he says quickly. "The police have Mark and his friend locked up in the city."

The policeman explains everything to the chief and the medicine man. Your uncle puts his arm around your shoulder and leads you to a waiting truck. You climb in and turn around. The bonfire where you were standing is huge now, and the post in the middle is burning brightly.

The End

You grab her arm. "No way!" you say. "I just over-heard someone say they were going to kill you and make it look like an accident!"

Maryanne and Ron exchange glances. "What about the blood?" Maryanne asks.

"Leave it!" you say.

The two of them stare at you, panicked expressions on their faces. "Follow me," you say. You race back toward the Land Rover, tearing through the tall elephant grass. Ron jumps into the driver's seat and starts the truck.

"Thank you," Maryanne gasps, still out of breath. "Mark assured us that because they thought he was one of them, we'd be safe."

It takes several hours to get back to the hospital. When you finally arrive, your uncle comes out immediately. "Where's Mark?" he demands. You tell him about your experience in the jungle.

"Oh, no!" Uncle Steve cries. "I'm sure he told those madmen you were scientists working with him. Your fleeing may mean his death."

"You mean he's really in the CIA?" you ask.

"Oh, yes, absolutely," your uncle offers. "Mojundi was buying Ebola-contaminated blood to be used as a weapon against Nuano. The CIA got involved when the president of Nuano realized what was going on. After all, an epidemic of Ebola could affect many nations."

Turn to page 36.

You climb into the Land Rover with the others who are going to Kimundi Cave. Burt has decided to take both Land Rovers in case one runs into trouble. The other group will hike to the wild zoo.

Julia sits next to you. You haven't seen Mark or Roloff yet. You hope they go with the other group.

It's a beautiful morning, and the all-day drive to the cave is uneventful. When you stop for a lunch break, Mark and Roloff climb out of the second Land Rover. They go out of their way to ignore you.

"See?" Julia says, her eyebrows raised. "I *thought* they'd follow us. My guess is they think we know something we don't."

After lunch, you all climb back into the Land Rovers and drive until you reach the mountains. Olive trees and cedars grow all around. The cave is located in a rain forest. A few holes and clearings in the forest allow sunlight to peek through.

You reach the area where you will camp in the late afternoon. Everyone helps to unload. You have been selected to be part of the team that will go into the cave the next morning and take samples. The other team members will set up a makeshift lab close to the mouth of the cave.

$\longrightarrow$

You rise before dawn and start building a fire. It's raining. The others are still sleeping. You can't wait to start, so you wake Julia, who is working at the makeshift lab today, and put on your sterile suit and helmet. Wearing a headlamp and carrying a flashlight and other gear, you enter the vast cave. You wonder what in the cave might be carrying the virus.

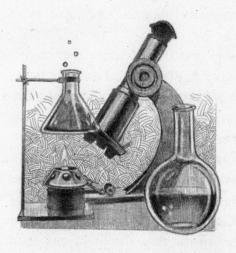

Turn to page 88.

70

"Our nganga is certain that all of you are involved in this conspiracy to eradicate our people. If enough are poisoned by the disease, it will be easy for Dictator Mojundi to take over our country."

"Wait," you say. "I knew nothing about this conspiracy until today. I risked my life getting this contaminated blood back from the enemy."

The chief speaks, and the man who captured you translates: "This blood belongs to us. We trusted you and your fellow scientists. Now we must have a ceremony and burn the tainted blood. Our medicine man believes that sacrificing one of the scientists with the blood will purify the air, and our people will be healed."

"But—but—"

The chief gets up and leaves. The giant takes your arm, and you follow him. You are furious.

The giant leads you to a small hut and ushers you in. A mouse darts across the floor, then another. *What if these are the Ebola carriers?* you wonder.

You are alone in a hut in the middle of a vast jungle. As the sun rises high in the sky, the weather becomes even hotter than yesterday. You sit inside the hut, dodging mice and praying for help to come.

At the end of the day, the giant comes for you. He takes you by the arm and leads you to the center of the village. A bonfire is burning there. The medicine man points to you and shouts something. The villagers raise their hands and shout back in reply.

Turn to page 23.

You need to ask Mark a question, but he's not there. Maryanne and Ron are finishing up. The medicine man follows behind them, placing cold, wet cloths on the foreheads of the sick villagers. Some of them continue to yell out or moan in pain.

On your way back to the center of the village, you stop and remove your protective gear, placing it in a plastic bag and throwing it over your shoulder. You continue on and find your translator sitting with the women of the village, munching on something. You realize that you haven't eaten since breakfast. You decide to check if there's any food left in the Land Rover from what you packed this morning.

Mark is sitting in the vehicle. It looks as if he's talking with someone. You duck behind a nearby tree so they can't see you.

It's the strange man from the airport! Where did he come from?

You sneak closer to the truck.

"I can take off and leave them all here," you hear Mark saying. "It would take them at least a week to get back to the hospital. *If* they made it."

"What about a radio?" the stranger asks.

"It's here." Mark chuckles. "I have the food, the blood, the radio . . ."

Turn to page 27.

"Mark Turner and Roloff Boulin frauds. Serious terrorists. Help on the way. Over."

You are about to reply when a loud gunshot report makes you nearly jump out of your skin. Mark has blown the radio set away.

"Surprise!" he says. "Now give me the blood. We'll take it all!"

Roloff grabs Julia's arm. "You come with us," he says in French. She tries to pull away from him.

You jump up to help her, but when you do, you trip and fall over the suitcase of blood vials—some with no caps on them. You feel a shooting pain in your leg. You look down to see that you've cut yourself on a sharp stone. Blood from the tubes is splashed all over you.

You lie there, listening to Mark laughing as he backs the Land Rover out. Julia's face peers helplessly from the window.

The End

You drop the box and run as fast as you can to the Land Rover. It's the only way you can escape the people chasing after you.

Finally you reach the road. The Land Rover is pulling slowly away. You look behind you and see no one. Your pursuers must have come upon the box of blood and decided to let you go. But now you know that Mark is involved in some kind of plot to destroy a whole country.

You chase down the Land Rover, shouting at the top of your lungs. When you are close enough to touch it, you bang on the back window. The truck comes to an abrupt halt. You are safe at last.

Maryanne jumps out of the vehicle. "We couldn't imagine what happened to you!" she says, hugging you. "Mark insisted that we go ahead and that he would find you. Where is he?"

Gasping, you try to explain everything that has happened.

"Calm down. Take a deep breath," Maryanne says. "Here, I'll get you some water."

She reaches into the back of the Land Rover for a container of water and makes you take a drink.

"I feel so bad," you say. "I had to leave the box of blood vials. I was so close."

Turn to page 24.

You glance toward the baggage claim and see Uncle Steve deep in conversation with Maryanne Ruggiero, a veterinarian who specializes in primates. The rest of the team is listening as they wait for their luggage and supplies. You purchase a small bottle of water and run back to Mark. But he's not there.

You start looking around and soon find him, further away from the baggage claim, talking to a dark-haired man with the brim of his hat pulled down over his face. The stranger hands Mark a leather bag. Mark opens it and reaches in. He doesn't notice you standing there. He pulls out a wad of American money, then quickly shoves it back in.

"Hey, Mark!" you say. Mark turns to you, looking both surprised and angry. The other man has pulled something out of his pocket and is holding it under his coat. "I told you to go over there," Mark yells, jerking his head toward the food and beverage carts. Your uncle, hearing the noise, starts making his way over to you.

"What's going on?" Uncle Steve asks.

"This one can't follow orders," Mark says fiercely, pointing at you. The strange man has disappeared.

"Come with me," your uncle says. As the two of you walk back toward the baggage claim, you wonder whether to tell Uncle Steve what you saw.

"Just stay out of his way," your uncle tells you sternly. "We have a lot of work to do."

Turn to page 37.

Maryanne smiles wanly. You know that their chances of surviving are extremely low. Once you are all suited up in protective gear, you watch as team members bring stretchers and lift the two scientists into the helicopters.

The End

"Mark is probably right," you say. "My vote is to head back to the city."

Ron shrugs. He checks the gas gauge in the Land Rover, and he and Mark take out the extra container of gas and fill the tank.

"What can I do?" you ask.

"Stay out of the way," Mark says gruffly. You look around.

"It sounds as if there's running water nearby," you remark. Everyone ignores you. You step through the tall grass, following the sound of the water. Soon you reach a river. You lean down and splash cool water on your face. It feels good. You can hear cicadas all around.

Just as you turn to go back to the Land Rover, you notice a light about a quarter of a mile downriver. You decide to check it out.

Hunching down so you're covered by the tall grasses, you make your way to the light. It's a bonfire. About twenty people are gathered in a circle around it. It is all you can do to keep from crying out to the others. Roloff, the stranger who stole the Land Rover, is there. He looks more sinister in the firelight. He is speaking to the others in broken English.

"We have ten captives from as many villages," he says. He motions off to one side. You can see the captives sitting in a group. They are tied to each other with rope. They look terrified.

Turn to page 12.

"Forget it," Mark says abruptly. "Nothing will help her now." You know that what he says is true, but it makes you angry. A crowd gathers. While you are standing there, the woman dies. Other women start crying and begin to gather up the body.

Mark goes over and speaks to them. You're surprised that he can make himself understood; he's the one who insisted on having a translator. The women stare at him, then rest the dead woman's head on a mound of moss.

One of the older women beckons for you to follow her up to a large hut. You hear more moaning as you approach.

Nothing has prepared you for the sight before you. At least fifteen people are lying there, in various stages of agony. Some are too far gone to even consider helping. Others cry out in pain.

Ron turns to the nganga. He acts out taking blood samples and asks permission. The medicine man nods. Ron looks surprised. Maryanne is already in her protective gear. She goes over to the first patient and efficiently draws blood. She puts the blood into a tube, labels it, and places it carefully into a box. After ten tubes are filled, you take the box to the refrigeration unit that runs off a generator in the Land Rover.

When you return, the nganga looks impatient. You can imagine how strange this invasion must be for him.

Turn to page 71.

Your uncle's voice interrupts your thoughts. "Mark?"

Mark looks around and smiles. He is proud that he can choose to work in any area. "I think I'll wait and see where I'm needed after everyone else has decided," he replies. *Rats,* you think.

Finding the source of the disease is like putting together a puzzle, or playing wildlife adventurer. Probably Frank Winston will lead that group. He isn't afraid of anything. As part of his team, you'd be collecting and testing everything from bats to insects to monkeys, trying to locate the origin of the virus.

Working at the hospital would be exciting, too, especially if they set up a hot zone lab. But it would be nerve-wracking as well, and you aren't positive that you can handle the pressure of the hot zone . . . or of being around so many dying people.

Going to the villages would mean meeting and interacting with the people of Nuano. You would interview families of patients, tracing the illness back to their villages. Again, there would be the risk of exposure to the disease, but also exposure to a new culture.

"What's your decision?" your uncle asks.

Go to page 98 if you want to pursue the virus trail in the villages.

Go to page 91 if you want to stay and help in the hospital and work in the hot zone lab.

Go to page 16 if you choose to go out into the field and find possible sources for the virus.

You decide you'd be better off going back to the hospital, even though Mark and Roloff will no doubt be there. "Artie, the only vial of that blood is in the Level 4 lab at the hospital."

"You're asking the impossible," Artie replies flatly.

"Take a road that circles around the city," you suggest. "And I'll figure out something from there."

"I just risked life and limb to get you out of there," Artie complains. "And now you're going back in through a different door."

As Artie starts to turn onto the dirt road behind the hospital, the Porsche is hit from behind, causing the car to lurch forward. "Mark and Roloff!" you gasp.

"Those creeps—" Before Artie can say another word, Mark, who is driving, bumps you again, this time a little harder.

"They mean business," Artie says grimly. "The hospital is at the top of the hill. Run for it!"

Before you have time to think, he drives the car off the road behind a huge clump of trees. "GO!" he yells. You jump out and dart behind the bushes. Artie starts moving, and Mark and Roloff turn around and begin chasing him again. They haven't seen you get out. As they disappear, you run up to the hospital grounds.

Turn to page 46.

You let the Land Rover go. Mark is standing there looking furious and a little frightened. "Now look what you've caused!" he screams.

"*I've* caused?" you ask. "We're stuck out in this village with no transportation and all these people dying. That guy has taken off with enough blood to start another epidemic!"

"Isn't your imagination running a little wild?" he asks.

You see Ron and Maryanne approaching. "I'll do the talking," Mark says emphatically. "You don't know what's going on, so just keep your mouth shut."

Either he's crazy or I am, you think. Maryanne looks tired. "I can't wait to get out of here," she says. "I'm not in the mood to eat snake meat."

Ron is right behind her. "Where's the Land Rover?" he asks.

Mark looks sheepish. "Stolen," he says.

"One of the villagers?" Ron asks.

You decide to speak up. "I don't think so. He had dark hair, and scars all over his face. He was wearing—"

Mark grabs your arm and squeezes hard. "This one wants to be a hero." He laughs. "If *I* didn't get a good look at the car thief, how did our hero here?" He laughs again. Maryanne is quiet.

Mark shrugs. "Sorry, guys," he says.

Turn to page 93.

You start backing down over the windshield onto the vehicle's hood. You can't take your eyes off Roloff's hand. He is holding a syringe.

You jump off the front end of the truck and start running as fast as you can. You can hear Roloff breathing heavily as he chases you. Something stings your neck. You slap at it, thinking—*hoping*—it's a bee. The last thing you remember is falling to the ground.

The End

"Amazing what money can do," he says. "You can get up now." You sit up. "We're going to my so-called office to see if we can get help. When those terrorists find you gone, you'll be in deep trouble."

Artie pulls up to a structure that looks more like a shed than an office building. You follow him. The minute he's in his office, he starts calling the States. To your amazement, he gets the CIA on the line, and it only takes a few minutes for him to convince them that he's for real.

The CIA tells Artie that Mark is not an undercover agent, and what's more, he was recently suspected of drug dealing. They tell Artie they'll have agents there within a few hours. Artie gets off the phone and looks at you. "I'll get you some food and water," he announces. "Don't turn on any lights. Just sit."

He walks out the door. You hear voices. Mark and Roloff! You have to make a quick decision. You can either go out and try to help Artie, or hide in the closet and hope Mark and Roloff don't find you in there.

If you hide out in the closet, go to page 19.

If you run out to help Artie, go to page 5.

Arriving at the hospital, you are shocked to see how dilapidated it looks. Weeds are growing in front of the ramshackle building. Inside, a nurse rushes over and speaks to Uncle Steve. He motions for all of you to follow. You are led into a room where the boxes of equipment and material have been stored. Silently, everyone slips into sterile gowns and masks. You follow Uncle Steve and the nurse into a patient's room. A woman is lying on a bed, staring into space. She doesn't blink or seem to notice when you enter. Two children are sleeping under the bed, and several other adults, probably relatives, are sitting on the floor.

Steve touches the patient's arm. Her eyes stare up at the ceiling. The nurse explains that the patient has been throwing up and complaining of a headache so severe it makes her want to scream. Your uncle tells the nurse to bring syringes. The nurse says something about the illness being malaria, which is what they are treating the patients for, but you know this is wishful thinking. The eyes of the rest of the team tell a different story: this looks like Ebola.

Even with your mask on, you feel like throwing up from the stench. The blood of the sick woman fills the vial of the syringe.

→

"What do you think?" the nurse asks your uncle.

"We're going to find out very soon," your uncle replies.

He hands the vial of blood to you. "I'll take more blood from other patients," he says. He asks Mark to take samples and have them shipped immediately to the lab in Antwerp and to Atlanta. Mark exits quickly.

Turn to page 31.

She points and tells you Uncle Steve is in Room 501. At the same time, she pushes a button that sets off an alarm. Two armed guards come running from the front door.

"Stop!" you hear. "Stop or we'll shoot!" You are within a few feet of Room 501. You turn, but it's too late for explanations. You hear a loud *bang,* and glass breaks as the vial of blood hits the floor. You feel a fiery, piercing sensation in your chest, then nothing at all.

The End

You manage to capture a flying squirrel, a spider, and a hyrax, a brown animal about the size of a woodchuck. Then, after collecting about fifty insects, you decide to take a break. When you emerge, you realize it is later than you thought. Julia takes the specimens and begins extracting blood from them. Two virologists are prepared with microscopes and other equipment to test the blood.

One of the scientists calls you over to his microscope. You close one eye and look through the lens. There it is! You look again. You recognize the shape of the virus that indicates Ebola. The blood sample was taken from the flying squirrel. "I've got it!" you call out. "It's Ebola!"

Abruptly Mark and Roloff yell out, "Freeze!" You turn around and stare at them. They are both holding guns! Suddenly you remember where you've seen Roloff before. He's the man Mark was talking to at the airport!

"We'll take that equipment and the flying squirrel," Mark says. "Quick!"

→

If they take the blood, the highly infectious virus will be in extremely dangerous hands. It would be like handing over an atomic bomb. And even if they don't plan to use the virus to kill people, Mark will make sure he gets all the credit for the discovery. Should you fight back and refuse to give up the virus? These guys have guns!

If you do as Mark and Roloff command and try to figure out how to stop them later, turn to page 95.

If you decide to risk your life and resist, go to page 17.

"Thought I'd come back and see if any food was left over from this morning," you say.

The stranger has been watching you the whole time. "Oh," Mark says. "Uh, this is Roloff Boulin, a virologist from France. He's offering to take the blood back to be shipped out."

"I'll come back for you," Roloff adds.

You see his face now for the first time. It is covered with scars, with what looks like a knife wound over the left eye. His eyes are bloodshot. His hair is coal black and slicked down.

"Ron probably won't allow that. May I speak to you alone for a minute?" you ask Mark.

Mark looks confused. He hops down out of the truck. "What do you want?"

"How come you haven't said anything about this man Roloff before?" you ask. "I don't think my uncle knows about him being here."

Mark suddenly looks furious. "Look, this man belongs here as much as I do," he yells.

A roar makes you both turn. The Land Rover is pulling out. You start chasing it, with Mark right behind you.

You can touch the rear bumper of the truck. You don't know whether to grab on or stop running and figure out some kind of plan with the others.

If you grab the Land Rover and try to stop the stranger, go to page 32.

If you stay and get reinforcements, go to page 81.

You decide to stay and work alongside your uncle in the hospital and hot zone lab.

Your first step is to isolate the hospital, preventing new patients from entering and sick ones from leaving. The next step is to quarantine the whole city. More scientists and doctors begin to arrive, and Uncle Steve is kept busy organizing everything.

You overhear him ordering some new arrivals to set up a temporary lab where blood samples can be analyzed. It will be tightly guarded, and anyone without a special badge will not be allowed near it. The rumor that the government of Chunga might have caused the epidemic has everyone on edge. A report has already come in that patients from ten different villages are registered in the hospital with symptoms of the virus. Considering how quickly a virus can be transmitted from person to person, it wouldn't take long to wipe out a whole population.

You enter the room where your uncle is examining a man brought in hours before. You have on the protective clothing and mask that all hospital staff must wear at all times. The patient is in the last stages of the disease. He stares into space, seeing nothing. His face is covered with a rash. You can see blood around his gums.

Turn to page 60.

He's in no mood to listen. "With all the work to do here, I have to get a report that you are selling contaminated blood?" he blurts out.

You're too shocked to speak. Mark and the stranger approach. You can see Artie out of the corner of your eye, taking notes.

"Never!" you cry. "Who is accusing me?"

Your uncle continues, "Mark and Roloff here—"

"They—they—" You're so angry you can't even speak. "That's what I wanted to talk to you about! Who is this Roloff guy anyway?"

"Roloff Boulin is one of the most outstanding virologists in the world," your uncle says. "He and Mark said they saw you dealing at the other end of the hospital. Then you ran out the door."

"But—"

Uncle Steve doesn't give you a chance to explain. "Ten vials of blood are missing from the Level 4 lab," he says. He sits down, suddenly looking exhausted, and puts his hands on his head.

"Are you okay?" you ask.

"Slight headache," Uncle Steve replies. "We'll have to have you arrested," he adds with a sigh. Three members of the medical team are standing around looking both anxious and angry. You notice two policemen behind the group.

Turn to page 58.

Ron looks worried. "The blood!" he says. "Whoever took the Land Rover is driving around with enough blood to . . ."

You pull your arm free of Mark's iron grip. He leans over to you and murmurs softly, so that only you can hear, "Say another word, and Ron dies." Then he speaks to Ron. "Chances are he doesn't even know it's there."

Ron turns to you with concern on his face. "Are you okay? You look like you've seen a man-eating cougar."

"I want to hike back," you say.

"Okay," Maryanne says. "I don't want to stay in this death pit either." She shudders. "It's awful back there."

Ron pulls his village map out. "We can get more supplies from the city, and another Land Rover, then head out to the next village."

"We have three cases that the medicine man claims he cured," Maryanne says. "If that's true, their blood will be like gold."

Your uncle has explained to you that scientists are experimenting with the blood of patients who have survived viruses like this to see if that blood may help cure others. Nothing has been proven, but having such antibodies for experimentation is a great help to the scientists. Because so few people with Ebola-like viruses live, their blood is very valuable.

You all go over to the chief to say good-bye. The chief makes a long speech.

Turn to page 18.

Mark gives you a dirty look. "It's insane to go into the jungle in the middle of the night," he insists. "Now let's all act like the rational scientists we are and get in the truck and go back to the city."

"I agree," Maryanne says.

Ron interjects, "This is our only chance to find the thief." He looks at you. "What about you?"

Panic rises in your throat. Mark has threatened that Ron will die if you say anything. It could be an empty threat; you don't know whether Mark even has a weapon. On the other hand, the thief has enough blood to contaminate a whole city in no time. Thousands of lives may be at stake.

"Well?" Everyone is looking at you.

If you decide it's safest to return to the city, go to page 77.

If you decide to risk Mark's rage and follow the footprints in an attempt to stop the stranger, go to page 25.

You decide not to risk getting killed. You may still be able to figure out a way to stop Mark and Roloff later. "Okay, okay," you agree. "But I want to remind you that the international police are aware of what you're up to, and you'll never make it out of here."

"Shut up and hand me that squirrel!" Mark demands. You look down at the squirrel in its cage. Julia had given it a relaxant before taking its blood, but it's beginning to wake up.

"Hurry up!" Mark yells. He is obviously nervous. The other scientists stand as still as statues. The squirrel is moving about now and making strange sounds.

"Take it to the Land Rover," Mark demands, gesturing with his gun.

You do as he says, placing the trap in the back of the vehicle. The two men follow you. Roloff shoots the tires out of the other truck. One of the scientists steps forward, and Roloff viciously shoots him in the foot.

Julia rushes over to help the wounded scientist as the first Land Rover roars off. A few seconds later, you hear a loud crash. You grab a pair of binoculars and see that the truck has hit a boulder and flipped over.

You and a few other members of the team run to the accident. Mark's head is covered with blood. He doesn't move. Roloff is slumped lifelessly in the passenger seat. A loud noise gets your attention. The little squirrel is jumping from seat to seat, screeching and chattering.

Turn to page 63.

You turn to the business at hand, which is to determine exactly what kind of virus this is. A blood sample from the same patient was shipped overnight to the Centers for Disease Control in Atlanta, Georgia, yesterday, but your uncle doesn't want to wait for their reply.

Mark has already extracted a tiny drop of the blood and placed it under a microscope. You do the same.

You study the sample for a long time. Your worst fears are confirmed. It's Ebola. You recognize the tiny circle with a tail. There's no other virus shaped like it.

You feel Mark's eyes on you. When you look up, he nods. Although you can't hear him through your protective helmet, you see him plainly mouth the word "Ebola." You suddenly feel as if you're about to faint. One spot of blood mixed with yours, and you're dead. One needle prick, and you're history.

Mark motions that he's leaving the lab and walks out. You follow, passing through decontamination after him. When you walk out into the corridor, he is nowhere in sight. You must find your uncle and tell him the bad news.

You head down the hall, searching the patients' rooms for Uncle Steve. Suddenly, you hear Mark's voice coming from one of the rooms as you pass. You quietly backtrack and peer into the room, trying to remain hidden. You see the same man Mark was talking to at the airport!

Turn to page 49.

You decide to join the group heading out to the village. Ron Winters is in charge. The morning after the big dinner, you help him finish loading gear into the ancient Land Rover that the Nuano government has provided for your use. You will help Ron locate the first person in the village to come down with the disease. He will also be trying to figure out how the disease is spread. Maybe he'll find someone who had the disease and didn't die. Their blood could help save the lives of those with Ebola.

Much to your dismay, Mark decides to join your group. You wish he had picked a different group, but on the other hand, this might be a good opportunity to see if he's up to no good.

At the last minute Maryanne runs up. "I can go with you for a couple of days," she says. You're happy to see her. She is always cheerful, and she can handle Mark's bad moods better than anyone else.

Nothing can put a damper on your excitement as you head out into the wilderness of Nuano. Maryanne holds up a canvas bag that she explains is filled with "goodies" to help win the local people over. Everyone laughs when she pulls out a toothbrush.

The sun beats down hard on the Land Rover, making you feel as if you're in a steam room. Mark holds a map that shows where the village is located. The road becomes almost nonexistent. Some of the ruts are so deep that you have to get out and push.

Turn to page 35.

"But it's Mark and Roloff," you say weakly.

"I know," Artie replies. "I'm running a check on Roloff back in the States. I can almost guarantee you he's not who he says he is."

"Then who is he?" you ask.

"I'm not sure, but my bet is he's working with Dictator Mojundi. Come on, we've gotta get out of here."

"We can't go out the window, and there's a guard at the door," you say.

"How do you think I got in? The guard went to get a drink," Artie smiles. "On the house."

"You paid him off?"

"Don't worry," Artie says. "Just stick with me."

You run out behind him. No one is in sight. Artie takes you through an unlocked back door. "Quick," he says. "Jump into my jalopy."

You climb into the backseat of Artie's Porsche, and he throws a raincoat over you.

He backs the car up and heads out. "Uh-oh," he says. "Security check. I'm cleared," he tells the security guard. "Here's my pass." There's a long pause. Your heart is pounding so hard you're sure the guard can hear it. The crowds are still yelling. Artie drives on.

Turn to page 83.

"Hey, folks," he says to those of you sitting in the vehicles. "Meet Roloff Boulin, France's leading virus hunter. I personally invited him. Hope you can squeeze him in." You wonder why your uncle never mentioned this guy.

Roloff climbs in next to you. "Good to meet you." He smiles. Something about him seems vaguely familiar.

Everyone introduces themselves. It is a long, bumpy, and mostly quiet ride to the cave. Everyone is thinking about the work ahead. Julia chats in French with Roloff.

At sunset, Burt finally pulls to a stop. It feels good to stretch your legs. The area you are in overlooks a large savannah. A light breeze blows through the tall grasses. The view is beautiful. You help collect wood to build a fire. Julia comes over and joins you.

"That man does not speak French like a true Frenchman," she whispers. "He cannot be French."

"But Mark says he's France's—" you whisper.

"Not this man," she says.

→

Your conversation is interrupted by Burt, who is making an announcement. "I've decided to divide us up. Half of us will go up to the cave for two nights, and the other half will proceed to a sort of zoo nearby. The owner captures animals in the wild. He might be able to help us find the source of the Ebola."

You glance over and see Roloff staring at you and Julia. "I smell trouble," she says.

If you decide to do your detective work at the wild zoo, go to page 21.

If you think you're more likely to find the source of the virus at Kimundi Cave, go to page 68.

ABOUT THE AUTHOR

R. A. MONTGOMERY is an educator and publisher. A graduate of Williams College, he also studied in graduate programs at Yale University and New York University. After serving in a variety of administrative capacities at Williston Academy and Columbia University, he cofounded Waitsfield Summer School in 1965. Following that, Montgomery helped found a research firm specializing in the development of educational programs. He worked for several years as a consultant to the Peace Corps in Washington, D.C., and West Africa. He is now both a publisher and multimedia developer.

ABOUT THE ILLUSTRATOR

ERIC CHERRY's first artistic influence was his father, a Washington, D.C., police artist who taught him the basics of illustration while finishing his sketches at the dining room table. Eric lives in New York City and studies under Frank Mason at the Art Students League there.